IN HONOR of
Katie O'Dell

THE
Library
FOUNDATION

Enhancing the work of our library
libraryfoundation.org

Three Magic Balloons

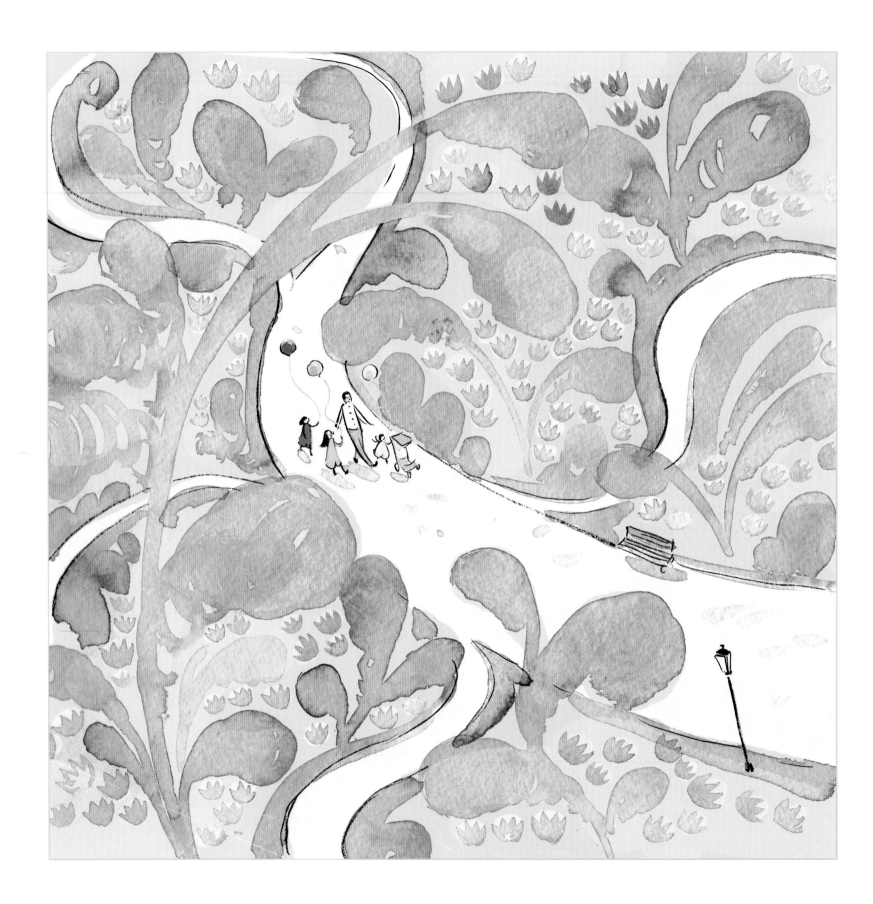

Three Magic Balloons

AS TOLD TO

Julianna Margulies *AND HER SISTERS,*
Rachel Mara Smit and Alexandra Margulies

BY Paul Margulies

ILLUSTRATED BY Grant Shaffer

Random House
New York

This book is dedicated to Paul's five grandchildren:
Kira, Chelsea, Marley, Jessie, and Kieran.
—J.M., R.M.S., A.M.

For my husband, Alan
—G.S.

Visit us on the Web! randomhousekids.com
Educators and librarians, for a variety of teaching tools, visit us at RHTeachersLibrarians.com

Library of Congress Cataloging-in-Publication Data
Names: Margulies, Paul | Shaffer, Grant, illustrator.
Title: Three magic balloons : as told to Julianna Margulies and her sisters / by Paul Margulies ;
illustrated by Grant Shaffer. Description: First edition. | New York : Random House, [2016] |
Summary: "Follows three sisters who take weekly trips to the zoo with their father.
Because the girls are so kind to the animals, a vendor gives them balloons
that carry them off to magical adventures at night"— Provided by publisher.
Identifiers: LCCN 2015023245 | ISBN 978-1-101-93523-1(hardcover) |
ISBN 978-1-101-93524-8 (hardcover library binding) | ISBN 978-1-101-93525-5 (ebook)
Subjects: | CYAC: Bedtime—Fiction. | Magic—Fiction. | Kindness—Fiction. | Animals—Fiction. |
Sisters—Fiction. | BISAC: JUVENILE FICTION / Religious / Christian / Bedtime & Dreams.
Classification: LCC PZ7.M3362 Th 2016 | DDC [E]—dc23   LC record available at http://lccn.loc.gov/2015023245

MANUFACTURED IN CHINA
Book design by Martha Rago
10 9 8 7 6 5 4 3 2 1
First Edition

About the Story

When we were children, our father always told us the best stories. Two of his children's books—*Gold Steps, Stone Steps* and *What Julianna Could See*—were published during his lifetime. Shortly after his death, we were going through his papers and found *Three Magic Balloons,* another story he had written for us when we were very little—one we had forgotten about. We agreed that this story needed to be read by children around the world, but only if we could find an artist who could capture his words in beautiful pictures. Grant Shaffer is a dear friend and a talented illustrator, and wanting to keep it close to the family, we gave him the story. Within days, his sketches were just what we were looking for, only better than we could have imagined.

Our father always told us, "Magic is everywhere. You just need to know where to look!" Our hope is that children will read his story and feel the same magic we did.

We would like to thank Random House for sharing our enthusiasm for our father's work.

With love,
Julianna, Rachel, and Alexandra

EVERY WEEK, Ariel, Miranda, and Jane went to the Children's Zoo with their dad. Winter, spring, summer, fall—it was always an adventure. One winter Saturday, their dad decided to give each of them some money and let them choose what present to buy.

It was certainly too cold for ice cream, and Ariel had plenty of candies in her bag. Should they buy toys? What about a balloon?

Then Miranda saw how the rabbits were shivering. Even the lambs, with all their fine wool, were cold. "I know," said Miranda. "Let's buy food for the animals."

Jane and Ariel agreed. So they put their coins in the machine for animal food and turned the handle. Out came little bags of food.

When Miranda saw how much the rabbits and lambs enjoyed it, she put some in her mouth and chewed. It tasted yucky.

From then on, whenever they went to the zoo, they bought food for the animals.

One Saturday in spring, when the daffodils were their prettiest and the cherry blossoms smelled their loveliest, the three sisters went to the zoo. As usual, they fed the animals. They had fun watching them eat, especially the rabbits, who wiggled their noses.

The balloon man came up to the girls, holding dozens of beautiful balloons on strings. "Sorry, Mr. Balloon Man," said Ariel, "but we've spent our money on food for the animals."

"I know," he said. "I have seen that you don't spend your money on yourselves. So I'm going to give each of you something magical."

The balloon man took three strings from his bundle and handed each girl a balloon. There was a blue one for Ariel, a red one for Miranda, and a yellow one for Jane.

"I want you to listen very carefully to what I have to say," said the balloon man. "If you do, you'll see something quite wonderful.

"Before you go to sleep tonight, tie the balloons to your beds very tightly. Then say your prayers and go to sleep as quickly as you can. Go now, children . . . and sweet dreams."

The girls thanked the balloon man. Dad tied the yellow balloon to a button on Jane's sweater. He found two sticks of just the right weight and tied Miranda's balloon to one and Ariel's to the other. Then they set off for home.

That night, Ariel tied the balloons to their beds. The sisters tried to go to sleep. Finally, their excitement began to wane and they drifted off to sleep. . . .

Ariel sat up. Her bed was rising gently from the floor!

She looked over at Miranda's bed and Jane's crib, which were rising, too. Both drifted slowly behind Ariel's bed, which was gliding through the open window.

Soon all three were floating above their
house, rising steadily toward the stars.

Ariel was standing, holding her headboard like the captain of a ship. Jane was standing, too, safe in her crib. But Miranda pulled the covers up to her neck, turning her head anxiously to look this way, then that. "Don't worry," Ariel called. "These are magic balloons, and nothing bad can happen to you." Soon Miranda was enjoying her flight high above the city, where she could see the twinkling lights spread out below like so many stars.

The magic balloons took them higher and higher, and closer and closer to the stars. They could hear music drifting toward them. And then they saw three angels. One was in a blue robe, one in red, and one in yellow.

The beds floated after the angels through a wonderful land.

It was like a garden, but no garden you have ever seen. The colors were alive and sparkling, and each plant was a wonder in itself, swaying and dancing in the sunlight.

Then all the heavenly animals came to meet the
girls. And this was even more wonderful. The girls had
never seen anything quite like them before.

The lion stood before them, all majesty and courage,
like a proudly beating heart.

The sheep was magnificent, too. Even as he stood there, he seemed to be in motion, sometimes appearing as the gentlest of lambs, sometimes as a great ram.

The girls wished they could give the animals something to eat, but they soon understood that the creatures didn't need food. They were nourished by the kind thoughts of children.

Then the angels began to sing, more beautifully than you can imagine.

"Join us," said the angels. And Ariel, Miranda, and Jane sang and sang and sang. Somehow they knew all the words to the songs.

It felt as if they had been there for only a short time, when Ariel glanced down at the earth and saw that the sun was rising over their city. "Oh, dear," she said to her angel. "We must return home before Mom and Dad wake up."

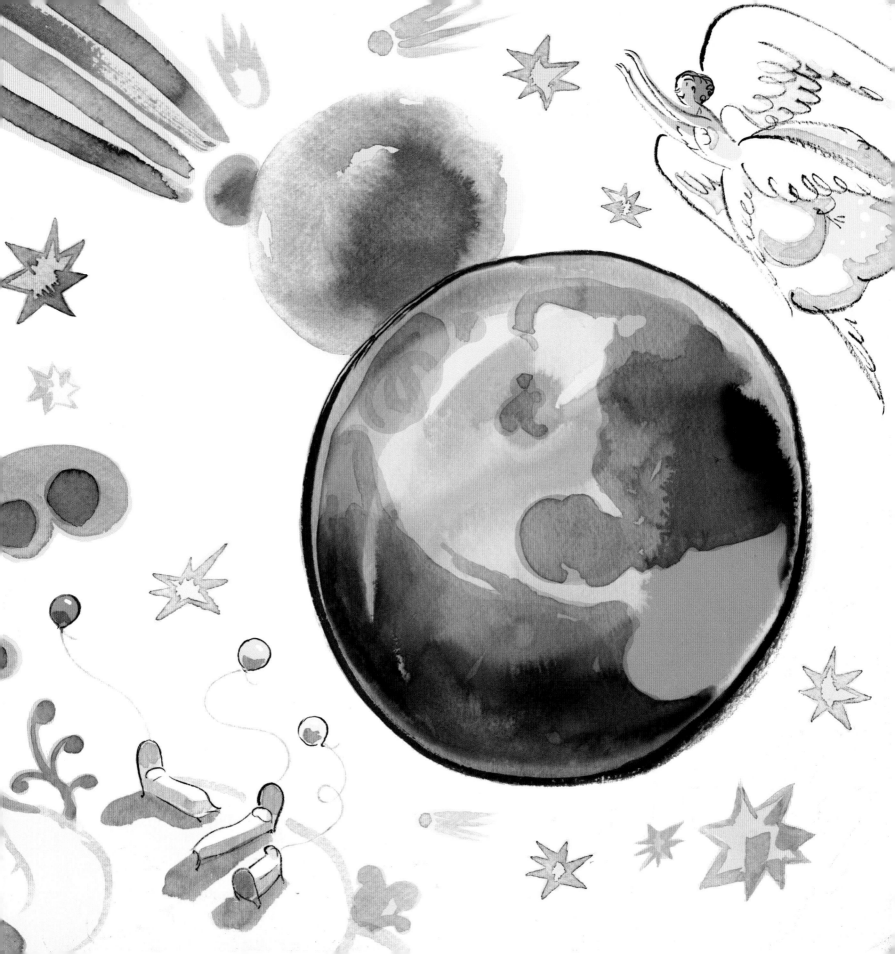

The angel nodded, went away, and returned with three long silver pins.

The blue angel, the red angel, and the yellow angel each touched a girl's balloon with a pin.

The air came out of them slowly, slowly, and each bed began to float back down to earth.

As the girls drifted, they heard the angels sing, "Goodbye, goodbye! We will be with you every day. You just have to know where to look."

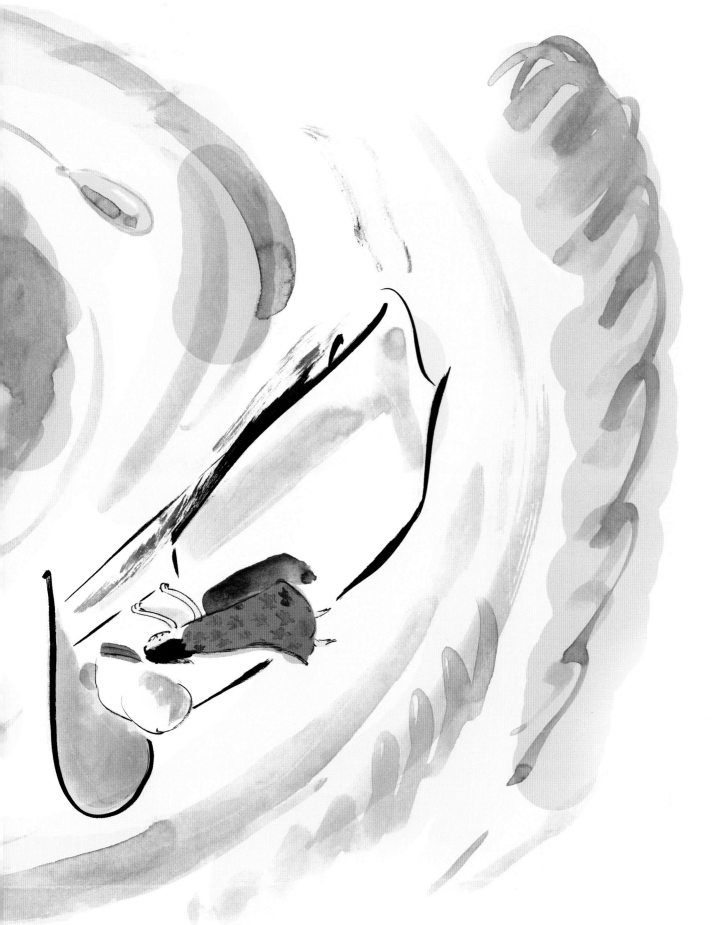

The sisters weren't the least bit tired, even though they had been singing all night.

Ariel suddenly began to worry. She noticed that the balloons were almost out of air. The beds began to fall faster and faster.

Just as it seemed they would fall—*kerplunk*—right out of the sky, the girls were surrounded by a whirring of wings. Blue jays and bluebirds from all over the world carried Ariel's bed gently through the sky. Cardinals and scarlet tanagers did the same for Miranda. And Jane's little crib was lifted by flocks of canaries and goldfinches.

Down, down, down, the birds gently flew the
girls and their beds right through their window.

And as swiftly as they had
appeared, the birds disappeared
through the window—*whoosh*—
in a fluttering of wings.

In came Dad, rushing to shut the window. "Good morning, girls," he said. "I wonder where that big wind came from."

"Good morning," said Mom. "Did you sleep well, my little angels?"
The girls looked at each other and smiled.

When their parents left the room, the girls looked under their beds.

Under Ariel's bed, there was a blue feather—as blue as her eyes, as thoughtful as the blue, blue sky.

Under Miranda's bed, there was a magnificent red feather—as warm as her kindness.

And under Jane's bed, there was a bright golden feather—shining like the sun in her heart.